THE HANGING TREE

A Novella

Michael Phillip Cash

Disclaimer
The characters and events portrayed in this book are fictitious. Any resemblance to real persons, living or dead is coincidental and not intended by the author.
No part of this book may be reproduced, or stored in a retrieval system, or transmitted in any form or by any means, electronic, mechanical, photocopying, recording, or otherwise, without express written permission of the publisher.

Copyright © 2013 Michael Phillip Cash

Published in the United States by

Red Feather Publishing New York – Los Angeles – Las Vegas
All rights reserved.

ISBN 10: 1492274518
ISBN 13: 9781492274513
Library of Congress Control Number: 2013915991
CreateSpace Independent Publishing Platform
North Charleston, South Carolina

Dedication

To Hallie & Cayla

Make it count.
- Michael

"It is our choices…that show what we truly are, far more than our abilities…"
J.K. Rowling

Follow Michael
@michaelpcash

www.michaelphillipcash.com

If you find this book enjoyable, I really hope you'll leave a review on Amazon under The Hanging Tree. If you have any questions or comments, please contact me directly at **michaelphillipcash@gmail.com**.

Praise for Michael Phillip Cash's debut book, Brood X: A Firsthand Account of the Great Cicada Invasion

> Simple, straightforward, flashlight-on-the-face campfire tale meant to induce nightmares." **- Mark McLaughlin - ForeWord Reviews**

> "Cash has written a harrowing tale of survival against all odds of a supernatural nature. As summer gets hot, *Brood X* will cool you down by sending chills down your back." **- Nina Schuyler, Author - The Translator**

> "Part creature-feature with all of the traditional elements of the great 50s films...part homage to the fairly recent genre of found-footage horror films-- *Brood X* is a quick, fun read." **- Michael R. Collings - hellnotes.com**

Michael Phillip Cash

"A Twilight Zone-like horror story of biblical proportions." - **Mark McLaughlin - Foreward Reviews**

"Horror at its best...up close and personal, and inflicted with ways that address humanity's inherent fear of and disgust for bugs." - **Mark McLaughlin - ForeWord Reviews**

"Breathing new life into a genre that has been occupied too long by the usual suspects: sickness, the undead and global warming." - **Kirkus Review**

- Critics love Cash's paranormal romance novel, Stillwell: A Haunting on Long Island

"Cash easily draws readers into the story by creating three-dimensional characters who are easy to care about...thriller meets love story in a novel where characterization shines...with strong characters and a twist unexpected in a thriller, this book is an enjoyable beach read." - **ForeWord Reviews**

"Michael Phillip Cash is creating a niche in the pantheon of successful young writers of the day." – **Grady Harp, Amazon Top Reviewer**

The Hanging Tree

"Stillwell has all the gothic type elements of the old great books with some of the new and satisfying elements that make it very readable and enjoyable." **– The Gothic Wanderer**

"A great read! Mr. Cash, I foresee more fast paced, thrillers in your future. A well written story with engaging characters." **–MyBookAddiction Reviews**

"Stillwell is a book that will keep you on the edge of your seat all the way through…it is one of the best books I have read in years." **– Chronicles from a Caveman**

"A horror tale with well-developed characters..." **- Kirkus Review**

"I do not see what would stop Michael Phillip Cash's horror masterpiece from becoming a bestseller." **- pjtheemt.blogspot.com**

Arielle

Oyster Bay, Summer-2013

The bark bit into the delicate skin of Arielle's back. Stars twinkled above her, dancing in the reflection of Chad's eyes. "Stop, really. Stop." She pushed at Chad's shoulders as he resisted her, his lips caressing the side of her neck. "I don't want to."

"Arielle, you promised,." Chad whispered, assaulting her lips. "I thought you said you love me," he wheedled.

Arielle looked at the leafy canopy. "I do. I really do, but I...I don't know if I want to do this. Especially here," she added practically.

Chad wheeled away, clearly annoyed, and bounced to his car door. The car was his pride and joy, a gift for his eighteenth birthday, a Camaro, light blue and totally awesome. It was a chick magnet, and for a minute he wanted to share that with Arielle. They had been dating for almost six months, and he was more than ready to take it to the next level. It wasn't his first time, and there were plenty of girls interested in him if

Arielle wasn't. Pulling a pack of cigarettes out of the console, he flipped a Zippo expertly, lit his cigarette, and inhaled deeply.

Arielle walked over and leaned against the car door nearby, moving close to him, trying to feel his moist body heat in the cool summer air. Crickets chirped nearby, and they watched traffic pick up on the road to the left of them.

"Looks like the movie ended," Arielle offered up some conversation.

Chad nodded but didn't respond. The silence stretched before them, anxiety building in her tight chest. She loved him, but this was big, huge; she just wasn't ready. She considered the spreading oak tree before them. Everybody was mad at her, everybody in the world. She knew she was going to be in hot water with her dad that night. He was pissed when she had walked out. She looked at Chad's profile in the dark, his features limned by the streetlamp. He was tall with sandy blond hair worn long and loose. It caressed his high cheekbones, and he was always brushing it from his warm, honey eyes. When he looked at a girl, she felt special. Well, he wasn't looking at her now, so she tried again. "They say the tree is haunted."

"I'm not afraid of ghosts," Chad declared, his wide mouth scowling. He wanted to punish her. There had been the promise for so long; he wanted to tell her to put up or he was out of here. She was one of the prettiest girls in the school, with hips that moved so gracefully he couldn't take his eyes off of her. The pale oval of her face gazed up at him, and he brushed her soft lips with his finger. She had the bluest eyes fringed by black lashes. Those eyes lit up with pleasure, and she rubbed her cheek against his knuckles. Picking up a light brown curl, he twined it around his fingers.

"Where's your penknife?" Arielle asked.

Digging into his back pocket, he handed it to her. She walked back to the tree, propped her foot against a large boulder at the base, and started to carve their initials into the chapped bark. She began with the C, but the surface proved resistant, and she broke out into a sweat, working hard to carve their names. Time stood still as the moon reached its zenith, clouds parting to let the fullness coat the earth with light. Leaves rustled as the wind skipped through the branches. Arielle heard a low hiss and stopped, looking over her shoulder. She scanned the deserted Long Island pavment, sighing gustily, and went back to her carving.

"So, Goody Bennett?" Arthur, a dapper man dressed in preppy clothing of another century asked softly from a lower branch, his voice the barest whisper. "Is she gonna give it up tonight?"

"What do you think, I'm a witch?" the ghost cackled, and the branches shook with mirth.

Laughter echoed in the still air, and both teenagers looked at each other. Arielle dropped the knife and ran to the safety of Chad's arms.

"Did you hear that?" she whispered, her face bleached of color.

Chad held her tightly in the security of his arms, liking it. "Must be coming from somebody's car further down. It's nothing," he replied more confidently than he felt.

"Let's get out of here," Arielle said, taking his hand, and tried to drag him to the car.

"Can't. Leo Manning said he'd swing by later. I have to wait for him."

Arielle frowned. She didn't like Leo. He was wild, drove fast, and had a bad reputation.

"Seriously? Leo? Why?" Arielle demanded.

"Why nothing." Chad threw his spent cigarette into the grass.

"I said I would wait, and that's what I'm gonna do."

Arielle pouted as she walked back to sit under the tree, her shoulder resting against the comforting support of its trunk. This wasn't going the way she expected. Chad was being weird. The whole night was strange. They were supposed to go to a movie then grab something to eat. Instead, there they sat, in the dark, waiting for Leo, of all people. She had defied her father even going anywhere that night. There were heated words, some raised voices, but she grabbed her new Louis Vuitton bag, a gift from her mother's boyfriend, and ran out the door. Her father didn't like Chad, didn't trust him, and had warned her he was not the guy for her. Arielle usually had a great relationship with her dad. He was the one she lived with, choosing to stay with him after the messy divorce. Her mom had run off to be with her boss, a rich Wall Street broker. Her father, a fireman with bum knees and close to retirement, was always there for her. She and her little sister, Charity, were his special girls. No matter how many great things her mother was able to buy her now, it was no match to the long hours her father had put in for school projects, cheerleading practice, and the rest. It was just… Arielle bit her bottom lip. She didn't like his new girlfriend, Belinda. Oh, sure, she was nice—you know that super-sweet, high-pitched-talking nice—but Arielle and her dad had less time together now. And Belinda acted like Arielle was always telling her the most amazing things on earth. Huh! She had the same expression for Charity and Grandma as well… so much for that. After all, Arielle understood that while her stuff was interesting, you could hardly say the same for her little sister or Grandma. That didn't translate well for ol' Belinda, she thought. So if he chose to be busy with someone Arielle didn't like, well, what did Grandma say? Something about sauce for the goose was good for the other goose or something like that. It all meant the same thing. She didn't have to like his choice, and he certainly didn't have to like her choice either.

"That wasn't very nice," a girl wearing a Gibson dress from the nineteenth century said as she peered down from her perch, looking at the top of Arielle's brown-haired head. She was timid and hid behind the foliage. "She's got nice hair. I wish I still had mine." She pulled at her shorn locks. They had cut her hair when she was ill and insensible. After the 'incident', she remember the parch burn of the fever, but she had to admit her memory of everything was hazy at best. She did recall the doctor's serious voice urging them to cut her hair as it was suffocating her, and perhaps that would save her from the heat of her temperature. Cringing, the young girl recalled the sound of them shearing off her auburn braids. It was a best feature, she thought ruefully. It made everyone sad, she could still hear her mother's mournful cries. Of course, nobody thought she could hear anything. She had been quite unconscious from the time of they brought her broken body home.

"He's not being nice because he thinks she's holding out on him," Martin's boyish voice added from a distant branch interrupting her pensive thought.

"How do you know that?" the girl responded.

"I'm a guy."

The girl sniffed at this, rolling what used to be baby-blue eyes, and he finished. "Well, I was a guy."

"That was a very long time ago, Martin. I do miss those days,"—this from the same branch of the tree, where the leaves grew more abundant. Sometimes you couldn't tell which one of the boys was talking. They even sounded alike with their clipped, New England, posh-school accents.

"If anyone shouldn't remember life, it should be me," Goody Bennett wheezed. "I've been here the longest. Coming onto three hundred and seventy years. I remember it like it was yesterday."

"Tell me about it," Gibson girl asked while she twirled a tight curl close to her head. She didn't want to think about the bad times, her bad times. "Goody, please tell me your story again," she pleaded, her voice sweet and youthful.

"Oh, no, not again," a new voice groaned. It was a female voice, world weary, beyond tired. It was a sad, raspy sound, as if the windpipe had been crush and never repaired. Gibson girl had trouble remembering exactly which one of her tree mates it was. *Let me see*, she thought. *There's Goody Bennett, the old cunning woman, Marty, and Artie, only they refuse to answer to that.* Mists cleared, and one could see they were a tangled mess, their legs twined together on the branch as if they were conjoined twins. You could tell them apart only because one wore a raccoon coat and the other a pair of goggles and a straw boater. *Who was that other spirit?* she pondered. She was distracted by Goody's voice.

"Let me think." Goody Bennett scratched her pointed chin. She had a dark mole on the tip that must have caused her major damage in her lifetime, Gibson girl thought. "It was the summer of forty-three or so when the problems began. Charles the First was king. He wasn't supposed to be…had an older brother who died. He was a weakling. Had no…what's that word?" she asked the other denizens.

"Charisma?" Arthur offered silkily.

"Exactly. Didn't know how to talk to people. No sense of style. Married a Catholic girl, he did. Made a lot of the people mad. Catholics…Protestants…doesn't matter much now, I know, but back then, whew…it was a whole different kettle of fish. Got his head chopped off too!" Goody laughed so hard she started to cough. "Now Charles the Second made a good king, sexy, had a fun court. Had lovely legs, that man…" She looked at Gibson girl's eyes glaze over. "That's not a story for you, gel. Let me go back to Charles the First. They were a stupid lot, especially his father, James the First. Hated witches. Wrote a book on them called *Daemonologie*. Stupid cur, caused a lot of trouble; that's why we left home."

The sky brightened and darkened, clouds moving backward, the sun speeding crazily in the sky. However, only the inhabitants of the hanging tree could actually see it.

Goody Bennett

Oyster Bay, Summer 1649

"Get thee blackberries, girl." Goodwife Bennett pointed to a patch of blue fruit growing under a ridge of bushes.

"Mayhaps there's a snake there, Grandmam. I am afraid."

The older woman pursed her wrinkled lips together, her mole more noticeable. "I've told thee many times, Claire, the snakes here cause no harm. They are our friends."

"Our friends!" the fifteen-year-old held her hand to her rosy cheek. "Surely not, Grandmam. Snakes can never be our friends. Think of Eve and what he made her do," she added in a shocked whisper.

Damn Reverend Harmond, the old woman thought angrily at the close- minded thoughts he was pounding into the young congregation's empty heads. "All God's creatures deserve respect." As if on cue, Remedy, her black tabby, agreed with a loud meow. Goodwife Bennett watched her granddaughter shudder and thought for once, *Why did my son's wife have to die and leave this child in my care?* They had left England four years ago, landing in this new community, her son succumbing to the fever almost immediately; her daughter-in-law passed eight months later, taking along the babe that refused to enter this new, wild country. They had left their small Dorset village among rumors of witchcraft, but whatever her healing power, it failed her dismally with both of them. She was a cunning woman, a healer. Her mixtures brought relief to the many people living nearby. They rummaged for herbs; she midwifed the people in their small town and in exchange had just enough to eat through the winter season. In summer they relied on the fish in a nearby brook and the small patch of vegetables that grew near the tiny stone cottage where they lived. The cottage had been abandoned by the previous family, who had been killed by Indians. A goat had wandered back, and so now they had a mean cottage with a scrawny goat that gave slightly sour milk.

"Be gone," Claire hissed to the cat, who calmly ignored her and walked on its feet daintily toward the underbrush.

"Like you the mice and vermin that come to share our very food?" Her grandmother banged her staff angrily. "Thanks be to have Remedy to rid us of pests."

"She's a foul creature, Grandmother. I do not like her."

"Go pick us some fruit now, child!" she ordered, following the younger girl as she skipped ahead. She did not have the strength to fight the ignorant girl anymore. Fanning herself with a leafy frond she picked from a tree, she wondered if she should just ask Adam Babcock if he wanted Claire for a wife. He stopped by often enough, and she observed his eyes follow her granddaughter around the room of the cottage. Mayhaps she should talk to him and see if she could get her married and off her hands.

The Hanging Tree

The sun beat down unmercifully, the rays persistent though their dark clothing. They walked down a steep ridge, where a giant oak tree shaded the scorched earth. A boulder had been rolled beneath the branches and Goody Bennett sat down, watching Claire roam the meadow looking for ripe fruit. Raising her thick skirts above her knees, the older woman enjoyed the refreshing breeze while her granddaughter picked happily at the blueberries. She was a pretty chit, *Aye*, Goody thought to herself, *I was just as slim and pretty too. Pretty doesna last forever*, she frowned looking at her own round belly, now resting comfortably on her lap. Glancing at misshapen, swollen ankles, she chuckled remembering them slim and attractive. *Not so pretty anymore, eh?* She thought to herself. *Mayhaps it's a good time to talk marriage with that young Adam Babcock before someone else notices empty headed Claire.* Butterflies floated on the sunbeams, birds chirped merrily, and she heard the familiar clip clop of a shod horse.

"Good morrow, Goody Bennett." The most honored rector tipped his black hat. He was a tall man; most thought him handsome. Goody Bennett found him whey-faced, but, she admitted ruefully, he had an amazing voice, booming like a deep kettledrum. He could be heard to the last pews in the church. A voice of warning, it stopped all traffic when he chose to use it.

Hastily lowering her skirts, she nodded back. "Reverend."

He frowned at the cat sunning lazily at her feet. Goody narrowed her rheumy eyes.

"You are far off the path, Mistress. What brings thee to these parts?" the reverend asked.

"We are hunting for berries. Claire," she shouted, "give good day to the reverend."

Claire blushed prettily, shielding her hands over her blue eyes, and smiled brightly upon spying the clergyman. He climbed down from the large roan mare.

He was tall, dressed all in black, and, while most expected him to be older, he was quite young, with a full head of chestnut hair. He was a learned man, attended Oxford, and was filled with bright ideas for this new country. The old ways and their superstitions had to be rooted out and burned away along with the witches that brought them. He could not help the smile that rose to his lips upon spying young Claire. Her budding breasts were taut against the outmoded bodice, her apple-colored cheeks vibrant against the white skin. She was lovely, with long blond hair tied behind the base of her skull to cascade down her narrow back. Sweetly she skipped toward them, her eyes on the reverend.

"Good day, sir." She peeked up under long lashes, her blue eyes glistening.

Her scent rose to meet him; he remembered that only last Sunday, when she edged close to him for a question, it tickled his nose. She smelled of the wild roses that dotted the trails all over their small village. How could so beautiful and pure a child come from this crone of a woman? His eyes rested upon the ugly mole at the base of the hag's pointed chin. The cat, certainly a spawn of Satan, meowed angrily, and Rev. Harmond cleared his throat. "Thee was missed at church Sunday, Mistress."

"I begged her to go," Claire eagerly interrupted.

"'Twas because of Goody Maywearing. She was laboring with her first child. I could not leave her thus."

"There is to be no labor on the Lord's Sabbath," the reverend intoned smugly.

"Tell that to the child begging to be born that day, kind sir. It was my Christian duty to help."

This was met with a harrumph as he mounted his horse again. They eyed each other warily.

"Make sure thee attend Sunday services this week, Goody Bennett. The Lord needs must make his acquaintance with thee, I think."

"I make my acquaintance with the Lord each and every day I live," Goody Bennett spit back.

"Grandmam!" Claire hissed. "We will be there, good sir. Good morrow." She waved gaily at his retreating back..

"I do not like that man." Goody Bennett muttered her narrowed eyes glistening fiercely.

Claire gasped when she noticed her grandmother's beady gaze glowing with the red heat of anger. It was no good when the old woman was angry. Claire shivered with fear coupled with resentment. It was because of her they had no friends. Oh, people called when they needed her cures. If an arm or leg was broken, there would be ham in the larder for a whole winter. But no one, save that dreadful Adam Babcock, stopped for tea. She resented his long looks. He was a dirty farmer. Claire wanted more. She didn't know exactly more of what, but she knew she just wanted more. Looking at her grandmother's evil stare, she crossed her fingers behind her back, warding off the old woman's spells, and replied, "Reverend Harmond is good and kind, Grandmother. He takes care of the poor."

"I do not see him doing anything for us." Her grandmother retorted grimly.

"He frowns upon thy herb mixtures. He has told us many times." Claire replied defending the good reverend.

"Well, when the flux arrives this fall, let us see how much he despises my potions," the crone dismissed the man, and Goody Bennett reached for some wild valerian to put in her many pockets.

"What plant is that?" Claire asked before returning to her search for the juicy berries dotting the underbrush.

"Never you mind," her grandmother responded harshly. "You stay out of my business, Claire. I be fair warning you."

The sun slid behind a purple cloud, and the air chilled. Fat drops plopped onto the dusty soil. Claire threw her stained apron over her hair and squealed with terror when thunder grumbled in the sky. She eyed her grandmother resentfully, wondering if the lightning that followed was due to some curse brewing behind the pursed lips. She ran ahead, not waiting for the older woman, her head ducked between her shoulders, stinging drops slashing against her heated skin.

Goody Bennett watched Claire run off and wondered again how her son could have created such a buffle-headed simpleton. Glancing back at Remedy, who bared pointy teeth, she rose, grumbling, "Aye, laugh thee silly fur off. I dinna ask for this, and thee know it!"

Together they walked back to their cabin, the cat gracefully leaping over small puddles, the old woman with a rare sense of doom.

"You knew what was in store for you, old woman." This was shouted from one of the tangled duo in the tree.

"As did you," she replied her ugly face split by a toothy smile. "We all know what is ahead for us, in one way or the other."

"If that was true, I would have never driven this road so fast," Arthur of the raccoon coat added.

"Ha! Did you not know the consequence of driving fast?" the old crone asked.

"Of course, but for everybody else. This was not supposed to happen to me," came the pithy reply.

"That's what they all say," Gibson girl offered morosely. "Pray continue. I want to hear the rest of your tale. It is quite diverting," she finished primly.

"Who cares?" This was from a dark body swinging on one of the lower branches. Gibson girl peered through the brush but couldn't make out the faint face. "We all know what happened. How many times do I have to hear this?" the specter wailed.

"Until they learn," Arthur whispered fiercely. They all looked down at Arielle's unsuspecting head.

Goody Bennett

Oyster Bay, Fall 1649

The days came and went with ruthless speed. Summer moved toward fall, and the old woman continued to help those who needed potions and perhaps a spell or two. The Indian summer scorched the earth, making harvest heartbreakingly scant. They were nervous, the small community. Stores in the town ran low, shipments stopped coming from England. Far from the civilization of New Amsterdam or Boston, they were the last stop for dwindling supplies. They had to make do with what they had, and they didn't have much. There was a revolution back home. The king was dead, a new protector, Oliver Cromwell, running the country. The people were unsettled; they didn't know what tomorrow would bring. War ravaged home, making supplies even scarcer.

The air was sultry, and the cows mooed in their pastures. Goody Bennett was exhausted. Sluggishly, she used her staff to walk home, Remedy trailing behind her. The door was open, and Claire sat outside churning butter. She watched her grandmother amble up the road, unhappiness written all over her face. "It is too hot to churn outside, Claire. Go in the house."

Claire shrugged indifferently. "Be thee hungry?"

"Nay." The older woman shook her head. "I have lost whatever appetite I have. Both Mother and babe have perished."

"Mayhap your magic is gone." Claire shrugged indifferently.

"What are you about, child? I have no magic." The older woman held up her gnarled hands. "I have need of knowledge, not magic. How do you help a babe who refuses to descend?"

She climbed the step to the dark interior, letting its coolness bathe her sweating face. It had been a long night, made longer still by the hopeless cries of her neighbor. Calvin Beckworth sat outside keeping his young son busy, while his wife labored the day and night away. She had trouble bringing forth the boy two years ago, and he had expected Goody Bennett to do her job and deliver of his wife a healthy child. Only, no matter how much she greased her hands with the sweet honey she had found on a shelf over the fireplace, or how many sharp knives she placed under the sheets to cut the pain, nothing helped Mary, and, as dawn melted the darkness, she quit this world for paradise, leaving the farmer alone with a toddler and no help meet. Goody left the airless cottage, her eyes watching Calvin Beckworth narrowed gaze. She felt his hostile glare on her stooped back, his anger pulsing with primal heat and she knew he was now a dangerous enemy.

What am I going to do now? Beckworth thought angrily. Though Goody knew his very thoughts, she could not assure him all would be well. If the eyes were mirror to the soul, Goody Bennett saw only dark hatred in their depths. *Who would watch the boy while he tended his harvest? Perhaps the old woman did not help as much as she could have.* She heard grief and ignorance in his words, but could not reveal that she could hear the

The Hanging Tree

words swirling in his head.. She could feel him wonder. *Where is my precious jar of honey?* I used it, fool, she wanted to shout at him. I used it to help your wife.

She remembered his suspicious eyes following her as she left defeated and dismayed at losing a fine young woman.

"What happened?" Claire asked.

"The babe refused to come out," was the curt reply.

"Mayhap thee should have attended services yesterday instead and both mother and child would have survived." Claire tartly informed her.

"What mischief is this, Claire? What arcane ideas have scrambled thy thoughts?" She pointed a crooked finger at her.

"The good reverend tells us to place our faith in God and not heathen magic." Claire shooed the cat with a broom; it hissed angrily at her.

Goodwife Bennett touched her dirty nail to Claire's pristine forehead. "These are wicked thoughts, child. I am thy blood. Be I a witch then so you be too."

"Nay!" Clair shouted, backing away. "I hate thee and thy potions. I am pure, an angel; the good reverend has told me."

"Does he say that when he caresses thy breasts, sweet, pure Claire?" her grandmother asked in a wicked whisper.

Claire gasped, her hand on her chest, her breath coming in short pants. *How did she know?* She thought wildly. They met in private, the good reverend and Claire, in the meadow by the large oak. They had lain together under the leafy branches. The sun warmed their bodies, and he spoke of her beauty and their future together. He was a good man, leading his flock, keeping them in the light of the Lord, guarding against evil. His loving hands caressed her, urging her to tell him the true nature of her family. How could she resist such a man? The grim cabin filled with witch's tools and the evil devil's familiar were of her past. She was impatient to disregard it for a future as the respected wife of the leader in their small community. He promised her she would have the best as he took her maidenhead. She was a siren; He told her. She seduced him with her beauty; He adored the purity of her body. They were destined to be together. He only needed to root out evil, prove himself the guardian of the community, save her from the darkness of her grandmother. It was her duty to tell him. Whispered words—the good reverend captured them with his tongue, lapping her secrets, promising brighter tomorrows.

"Where's thy good reverend now?" Goody Bennett cried, taking in Claire's wild face. The child protectively covered her blossoming belly. "Oh, aye promised thee the world, did he?" she accused, her black-cherry eyes boring into her granddaughter.

"Stop looking at me!" Clair wailed. "You...you witch!"

"Shhhhh..." Goody grabbed her by the lace collar; the girl was devoid of color. "Does thee want to be burned?"

"Me?" She shrank back, laughter bubbling up. "They won't burn me." Claire shook her head, her face red with shame. "I am not a witch. Thee are corrupt, foul...thee and your familiar, the devil's tool. George will test thee; he has no need to test me."

Goody Bennett pushed her away. "What have thee done, you pestilent child? What have thee started? You think you are safe?"

Grabbing her staff, the old woman ran from the cottage, Remedy hot on her heels behind her.

Peter

2013

"I don't like it. She just left. I don't understand her."

Pete took two cups of tea and brought them to the table toward his girlfriend. It sounded strange, a grown man having a "girlfriend." He looked at Belinda, who was calmly making room on the cluttered table. She cut him a piece of pound cake, took a quarter for herself then made another plate.

"Charity," she called his younger daughter. "Do you want ice cream with the cake?"

He smiled at this hominess. Why couldn't Arielle see how sweet and unpretentious Belinda was? She worked at the Cold Spring Harbor Laboratories. Ha, he landed himself a rocket scientist. Well, really a biologist. It was pretty funny, the fireman and the genetic mutation expert. They had met at the hospital. She was there bringing her father in, acid reflux that looked like a heart attack. He was there for Charity and the five stitches she needed after she collided with a baseball. Arielle had been beside herself. He almost thought he'd have two patients on his hands that day. She was so close to her sister, and yet she'd been pretty close-mouthed about the Chad boy. He didn't like it, not one bit.

Charity walked toward him, her braids messed, wearing a sloppy tee and sweats she slept in. "Is it vanilla?" She was petite, like his wife, with a small upturned nose he loved to tweak.

"Yup." Belinda got up to take out the Haagen-Dazs from the freezer. "I love this one. It's got chocolate-covered almonds in it. It's really good. I'm going to toast the pound cake and put the ice cream on top. You're going to looooove it!"

Charity slid into the seat next to her father and looked over his hand to see what was in his cup.

"Tea." He showed her. "You want a cup?"

She shook her head, pointed to his, and he slid it over to her with a sigh. "Just want a sip." She blew on the steaming liquid.

"Did you hear from your sister?" he asked as she returned the cup.

Charity nodded. "A few times. Did you?"

They were all on the phone constantly with each other. They always knew what the other was doing and where they were. They included their father; he must have spoken to his kids a dozen times a day. He was used to knowing everywhere they went, any hour, but something had shifted, and he just didn't understand why.

Charity glanced at Belinda, who was at the counter waiting for the toaster oven to bing. "She'll be fine," his daughter whispered softly. "I bet she comes home in a few hours and tells you you were right."

The Hanging Tree

Pete looked at the ceiling, his eyes smarting. It was cozy in the kitchen. He gazed at the worn tabletop, the four chairs, and felt an overwhelming feeling of loss. Someone was missing, someone important. Arielle, Charity, and Peter hardly missed a beat when Amy left. Though he worked in three-day shifts and was away, Amy worked from six in the morning and rarely got home before nine at night. His mom and an au pair named Julie did the bulk of the work. They had stopped doing everything together; her job pulled her more and more into the city. Amy and he had drifted until, one day, his wife just stopped coming home. He took a leave and gathered his girls, trying to regroup and let them know it wasn't about them. It was her boss, the lure of living in an expensive penthouse, going to society events. Amy didn't want to be there anymore. She called him and said there was nothing for her in Long Island; her life shifted to Manhattan. The girls could come, of course; if they really wanted to, she told him to let them know. But she understood if they didn't want to leave their comfort zone. It was an "unvite" if he ever heard one, and he couched it in a way more positive note when he explained what was going on. Arielle shrugged and told him she was too involved to even think of leaving school; Charity turned her very knowing eyes to him and silently shook her head. He knew there would be damage, but he didn't understand it would be like this. Arielle always shared everything with him, and he didn't understand why she suddenly became distant. For some reason his brain didn't register that his relationship cooled with his daughter as it heated up with the new woman in his life.

Arielle

"Don't touch it, Arielle!" Chad shouted.

"Oh, it's such a sweet kitty," Arielle said as she held out a soft hand.

"It could have rabies. Aside from that, it's all black."

"Really, Chad? Black? What are you, superstitious?" The cat picked its way sinuously through the tangled roots of the old tree to sit next to Arielle. Stretching its velvet body, it rubbed a lean back on the girl's knee. "Sweet cat." Arielle felt the gentle purr underneath the soft fur. They leaned back against a large bolder that had been propped against the tree.

"Look who's here." Right above them Arthur announced softly from the dense foliage, so faintly it sounded like a puff of air.

Arielle heard only the delicate whine of insects too close to her ear.

Goody Bennett sighed sadly. "Remedy..."

Chad sat down next to Arielle, reaching out to pet the cat. The animal arched, spitting furiously at him, scampering through the low bushes behind them. "Creepy."

"You scared her," Arielle accused, wondering what made the cat react to her boyfriend.

Goody Bennett

Winter 1650

A crowd was outside the cottage. Snow dotted the grounds; the frigid air pierced their lungs. They were loud and angry.

"My babe died."

"The cow's milk stopped."

"The corn is spoiled."

Claire parted the curtain and watched the villagers hurling rocks encased in ice at the door.

Calvin Beckworth was in the front, his hand wrapped around a rock that he shook angrily while he shouted. Goody didn't want to hear his thoughts now. She didn't need too, she could feel his hatred with his purple face and spit speckled lips.

"Get away from the window," Goody yelled. "They will leave soon. It's too cold for them to stay."

Claire sniffed and lumbered away from the door, her belly big and cumbersome. "Where is the righteous Reverend Harmond now?" Goody asked evilly.

It had gone on for them thusly through the long pregnancy. Claire defended her lover against her grandmother, and when it became apparent that he would not claim the child, she sank into a depression. Now her blond locks hung lank around her dull face, her skin pasty, and her blue eyes sunken.

"He will come. He told me he loves me."

"He called thee a succubus, handmaiden of the devil," the old lady responded with a cackle. "He will not come, Claire. Put him behind you." Goody Bennett thought back to that night almost five months ago when they sat in this room, a roaring fire painting their faces orange.

"Come now, Reverend, do right by my girl."

"Thy girl, thy girl..." He backed away from the two women, his face crimson in the firelight. "You sent her to seduce me. She is evil, the devil's tool."

Goody's eyes narrowed, and she took a long pull on her pipe. "Did thee think my Claire a devil's tool when you played with her pretty titties, good sir?" She pointed the stem of her pipe at him. "You took what didn't belong to you, and it canna be returned. You must make good on what evil you did."

"Evil?" Reverend Harmond shrieked. "Me? Evil? I know what you are, Goody Bennett. Soon all will know you for thy witching ways. I will see thee in hell first, old woman!"

With that, he swept out the door letting it slam so hard it shook the very roof of the cottage.

"Aye. I will see thee in hell, good sir," Goody agreed to the empty spot.

After that, slowly Goody Bennett's services were needed less and less. Villagers shied away from them. The supplies in their larder became scarce, and they stopped attending church altogether.

They were hungry and alone. Every so often a crowd gathered by their door, like this day, and hurled insults.

The Hanging Tree

"I cannot. I cannot go on." Claire sunk onto the hard-packed floor. "He promised me—" she continued in a singsong voice.

Goody Bennett took her pipe and sat in her rocker. The girl was losing her wits. She held out her arms, feeling pity for her. "Come, child. Rest thy head. You have naught but me now."

Claire looked at the mean room, the dirt floors, dried weeds hanging from the rafters. She felt the mound of her child moving under her dress. "There were supposed to be balls and parties. We were to have his father's house. He could not have lied."

"Why? Why? Because he is a man of God? Child, child, he is still a man, just a man with a man's needs. He does not care; he never did. He promised you so he could get what he wanted."

"What he wanted I gave freely. I love him."

"Thee speak of love?" The old lady laughed. "He did not want thy love, child. He coveted thy body. He wanted to know of our old ways, our cures.. Aye," she sighed. "And thee gave it freely."

"Nothing has happened, Grandmam."

"Aye. Nothing yet," she replied grimly.

Arielle

"They call this 'The Hanging Tree,'" Chad said as pulled Arielle closer to him and tried to kiss her again. He knew what he wanted, and was getting impatient waiting for Arielle to make up her mind. She had teased him for so long. Though he was confidant, Chad felt jumpy, his hands fidgety. She was beautiful, the star shine and moonbeams painting her lightly freckled cheekbones. She had a perfect nose that complimented a full mouth; he was the envy of all his friends.

"Why?" She dodged him.

"Not sure. I heard they used it to hang people in the olden days."

"It's so peaceful here. I can't believe that."

"Why? Do you think you'd be able to feel something, like it would be special or something?" Chad replied as he stood up laughing. Reaching up, he attempted to grab a low-hanging branch.

"Should I do something?" Arthur whispered with gleeful anticipation as the spirit took note of the foolish mortal. His broken jaw rattled with mirth, his eyes sightless in the broken face.

"Humph. These young people are so full of themselves." This was from Martin, ever the serious one of the two.

"Insufferable," growled a voice from the bottom branch.

"Why don't you ever show yourself?" Arthur pleaded. "We've shared this spot ever so long. I want to see you. Know your story."

"Can't," came the whispery reply.

"She can't," Goody answered. "She's stuck where she is, same as us."

"You can move."

"Well, yes, I can." Goody laughed. "I chose to stay here!" She stood balancing herself on the branch, swaying dangerously. "I will stay here until my job is done."

"What job?" Gibson girl asked. "What job?" She never understood half of what they were talking about. They all spoke in riddles. Instinctively, she knew somehow they were all protecting her, but from what, she just couldn't remember. It was always so hazy. Just out of her reach. Stretching for distant recollections, she only felt loneliness and pain. So much pain, faint memories nagged her. Distracted, she never heard the rest of the argument. Her boney frame shivered ever so slightly.

"She is staying here for revenge—nothing but revenge— and we are the results of her revenge!" Martin shouted back. Though he was attached to the tree, he bunched his shoulders and made an attempt to rise. His face glowed red, and if he could have, he would have been sweating with the effort to go after the witch.

"Stop, Marty," Arthur urged, his voice soft.

"Don't call me that!" Martin blasted an icy stare at his partner. "I hate when you call me that! I hate her! I hate this place!"

"Stop! That's why we are here. I won't leave you. You have to calm down." Arthur said fiercely, as if that's all Martin needed to hear.

The Hanging Tree

The air crackled with electricity, the silence thick to their ears. Arielle turned to Chad, whispering, "Do you think this place is evil? We would know it, right? We could feel it, don't you think?"

"If this place were evil, I would cut down the tree!" Chad sprang up, unnerved. They would know it, wouldn't they? Chad felt different there. His muscles pulsed with an energy he didn't understand, like he drank too many of those energy drinks. His blood felt thick, sluggish in his veins; he was aroused. He looked down at Arielle, his eyes narrowed, considering what he would do with her. His thoughts felt foreign, yet he didn't try to stop thinking them.

A chill danced down Arielle's bare arms. Chad looked strange, as if he were someone else. Someone she didn't know. Suddenly, she felt the urge to go home.

"Oh, are you afraid?" Chad gained purchase on the limb and swung back and forth. "Help me, Arielle," he wailed. "I'm hanging. It's got me."

"Stop Chad," Arielle smiled at his boyish antics.

"Oh, this is too much!" Arthur closed his eyes and commanded, "Hand!" An image of a ghostly hand reached over from where it lay detached from the mangled body and clawed its way to the end of the branch. The fingers stretched, responding to the command from the ghost. "I said attack. Now!"

"Stop, fool. You'll scare them!" Goody Bennett cried.

"As if you've never done anything to them. Pompous bastards." Arthur shouted back.

The hand grabbed the boy's prone fingers, tearing viciously at them. Chad screamed in horror, trying to let go, but was held fast. "Help me," his voice came out in a shriek.

He reached up, slapping at the air, and the chuckles died in Arielle's throat. "I'm not kidding. What the hell is up there?"

She ran over, grabbing his lean waist, but he was attached to the tree.

"Let go, Chad," she screamed.

"It's enough, Arthur. Let him go," Martin quietly demanded, his frustration and anger spent.

"You never let me have any fun, Marty."

"Martin. I told you Martin. Don't patronize me. They're children. You're really scaring them. I said stop it."

"Oh, all right, killjoy." Arthur turned his head almost completely around and ordered, "Release."

The hand dissolved into the night, and Chad fell clumsily to the grassy floor.

Arielle crouched down beside him. "Lemme see." She held out her hand to him.

He placed his hand in hers. "I don't see anything. What was it?"

"Ow, that hurt." He looked at the blossoming red scrapes on his knuckles, blood welling in the scratches. "Look, I'm bleeding." He held out injured fingers to her.

"What do you think it was?" Arielle came closer, inspecting his hand.

"I don't know."

"I didn't see anything. Do you think it was bugs? Maybe you disturbed a hornets' nest."

"Hornets don't fly at night, Arielle. Maybe we should move the car." He looked around for a better spot. He cast a worried look at his vehicle.

"The bark was very rough," Arielle suggested.

"Something scratched my hand." He rubbed his bruised hand against his shirt.

"We should get out of here. I don't like it." Arielle's eyes were wide in her face.

"Smart girl." Whispered words fell from the branches, the silence broken by the rustle of leaves. Only the teens never heard them. They looked up to see a bird hop onto the branch; relief replaced their fear.

"Oh, it was a bird. You were probably too close to its nest. Let's go home."

Chad sighed, feeling like his old self but smaller. "I can't. I promised Leo."

Goody Bennett

Late winter 1650

Hands pounded on her door, waking her from a deep sleep. "Claire," she whispered to an empty room.

"Goody Bennett." The door swung open. A man stood breathlessly in the doorway. He wasn't wearing a hat and looked distressed.. "It's Claire. You must come."

It was their only friend, Adam Babcock. He alone brought them game birds and rabbits through the long winter.

"What has happened?" Goody demanded, but Adam already had vanished out into the early morning.

Throwing on her shawl, she clumsily laced her shoes, fear taking residence in the pit of her empty stomach. A feeling of despair overwhelmed her. "Remedy," she called for her cat but received no answering meow. The cabin was cold and empty; puffs of frost formed before her mouth.

They trekked together silently through the dark meadow, the worn shawl little protection against the wind that pierced her skin.

"What is it?" she asked breathlessly.

"I was coming back from the pond. I cut through the meadow. Oh, Goody Bennett, I am sorry that—"

"Aye, thee is a good man, Adam Babcock." With dawning sadness, she knew already. Goody Bennett could hear the piteous wails of Remedy, the message loud and clear. "Say no more. I know what hath happened."

"How? How could you know, Mistress?" Adam asked. "I only just saw her."

Goody didn't answer. She didn't have words. Hanging from the lowest limb was Claire, her face blue, blond hair a curtain covering her bulging eyes.

Remedy circled underneath her, her cries loud, the truth written on the wind.

"What say thee?" Goody crouched low and listened to the cat..

Adam Babcock's mouth opened wide. "Nay, Mistress, cats cannot speak. Stop, I implore you, stop thy nonsense."

"He did?" Goody Bennett ignored him and kept addressing the cat. "He promised her what?"

Sitting down, she urged the cat closer. It purred as it climbed into her waiting arms. "I understand. You saw it all."

"Thee must stop," Babcock implored.

"Stop what, Master Babcock? Stop the proof that Goody Bennett is a witch?" a voice boomed from behind the tree. Tall and imposing, the good reverend stepped in front, and a group of villagers, mostly men, filed out from the bushes. "You heard her, good people."

"Kill her," Calvin Beckworth moved to the front, his face mottled with hatred and anger. "She be a witch. She killed my Mary."

The Hanging Tree

Cries erupted from the crowd and she heard their thoughts jumbled in her head.

"Hang her with her slut of a granddaughter." Beckworth moved towards her, his face evil in the firelight of the torches.

The reverend's eyes glittered with purpose. "She is damned and we'll all be damned with her, if we don't destroy her!" he shouted.

"You killed her, sure enough." Goody Bennett stood and pointed a gnarled finger at him while the cat rubbed itself against her short legs.

"I...I... You accuse me? With what evidence?" Harmond asked incredulously.

"Thee lured and seduced her with promise and got her with child," Goody spit, her eyes hot pits of coal. "Then when she came to you last night, thee brought her here and hung her." Her black eyes bore into him, and the reverend shivered. It was like a bottomless pit of hell. She was pure evil, and it was his job to rid her and her spawn from the community.

"Crazy witch...crazy old woman," Harmond howled back. "How come these revelations to you?"

"Remedy!" she shouted. "Remedy saw it all and told me. I know all of thy wicked deeds." She pierced him with her bold stare.

"Thy familiar. Thy cat that you suckle with the mole on thy chin! Evil wench! Dare you accuse me?" His voice echoed in the meadow.

"I accuse thee, Reverend George Harmond. Not only that, I curse thee, thy children and thy grandchildren, and their children after that. A curse will be upon your head, and I will wait in hell for thee." She pointed a crooked finger at him.

"Until you right this wrong, until you clear thy soul, thee and thine shall be cursed."

Crude hands hustled her onto the boulder under the tree. Her feet slipped, but fingers like talons held her in place as she felt the bite of a hemp rope.

Her hideous gurgle matched the wails of Remedy as the cat was strung up next to Goody Bennett. She watched her cat swing at the end of a rope, her face caught in a feral snarl. It's frantic cries becoming fainter and fainter. The sky darkened, mists rolled in, and the sound of the Reverend Harmond's voice became nothing more than a drone of bees on a summer day.

"So what happened to Claire?

Claire…where is she again?" Gibson girl asked.

"Oh, here we go. How many times do I have to tell you? I'm right here," Claire called from a lower branch. "Arielle," she called faintly, "leave this place."

Arielle

The cell phone's ring burst the night air.

"Dad?" Arielle answered the call. "Yeah, I'm with Chad. Um…no, the movie was boring." Chad moved away from her, lighting up another cigarette. "It's early," she whined. "I don't want to. We're hanging out. Just hanging out. I won't. Uh-huh, un-huh. All right," she hissed. Arielle was silent for a few moments, her voice resentful, her eyes glistening with tears. "Okay. I said okay. Bye."

"What did he want?" Chad asked grudgingly. "Do you have to go home?"

Arielle shrugged, her eyes downcast. "Soon. When is Leo going to get here?"

Chad looked at this cell and noted the time. "Should be here in any minute."

Arielle stood and brushed off her pants. "Maybe you should just take me home."

Chad's face darkened. "If you want to leave, call your old man and have him pick you up. What did he say: you're too young to be out with me?"

Arielle didn't answer, so he continued. "He is so going to ruin your life, Arielle. Your dad is too controlling."

"He's just watching out for me."

"He's gothic. Everybody is out. Look, you won't drink, you don't smoke, and you are the only one who won't smoke weed. Let me tell you, Arielle, most of us aren't going to take it for much longer."

She wanted so badly to be accepted. When her mom had left to move to the city, Arielle had been crushed. Even though they weren't close, she was her mom and a constant in her life. They didn't spend much time together. Arielle couldn't understand what she saw in her boss. Well, for that matter, she couldn't see what her father saw in Belinda either. Why were her parents so consumed with sex? Why couldn't they be like other parents and worry about things like ball games or shopping in big-box stores? Sighing, she admitted she liked her dad. He was always there for her. Except when he was on duty, and she understood that. Then Grandma pinched-hit. She was a character, and Arielle adored her. Her mom had the reverse role that most her of friends had with their dads. They breezed in and out of their lives, working long hours to support the families. She always knew her mom had a really important job and made way more money than her dad. He didn't mind and was happy she found something she loved—only nobody expected her to love it *that* much! It had been a hellish week. Mom announced she was moving with Tyler to LA. She and her sister could come and visit sometime next year. Her whole life was decided without her even being a part of the discussion. What if she didn't want to stay in New York? What if she preferred her mom to her dad? It seemed her opinion was not important, and, for that, Arielle was still mad at both of her parents. She had started hanging out with this crowd about then. Her pierced nose followed, along with a small tattoo on her right butt cheek that no one knew about. They were small rebellions, petty punishments for being ignored. Now she was on the verge of going all the way with Chad not because she liked him, she admitted finally to herself. It was a way to get back at her parents, let them know some decisions were hers and hers alone.

Martin And Arthur

Oyster Bay, 1915

"I don't want to go to school there!" Martin whined, throwing his napkin on the elegant dining table.

"Martin Pace," his mother drawled, "this display will stop instantly. Your Uncle Clive went to great lengths to get you into Harvard Law. You will finish what has been started for you." She gestured for the platter of cooling cutlets to be taken away.

"I don't like it, Mother. I want to join the army." Martin stood before a Turner landscape that took up a whole wall of the dining room.

"Really, Margaret." His stepfather took out an elegant pocket watch. "The histrionics are the height of selfishness. I have had enough of this drama. First Eugenie—"

"Why does he have to bring me up?" the eighteen-year-old debutante cried out, tears gathering in her silver eyes.

"A chauffeur, Eugenie?" His bulldog face turned to her, his protuberant eyes filled with disgust.

"Why don't you take an advertisement in the newspaper and announce it to the world?" the young girl asked dramatically. "You're despicable!" she hissed. Bending over, she picked up a black cat that was purring under the table.

"I hate that cat. Eugenie, I asked you to get rid of it," her stepfather complained. "It's a wicked animal."

"Wicked?" Eugenie screeched. "What do you implying?"

"Take what you want from that," he stepfather replied, his bulging eyes boring into her. "You live in *my* home, you eat *my* food…"

"*My* cat belongs to me, and you have nothing to say in the matter!" Eugenie took her pet and left the dining room.

"You will go to school, Martin; you will like it, and you will finish it. You have no choice, as did your father before you." Mrs. Harmond turned to her son as if nothing had interrupted the conversation. She could be quite oblivious when it suited her.

"Oh, he had a choice, Mother," Martin answered her. "He made his choices."

"We will not discuss your father's death," his mother's full lips trembled.

"The subject is closed. Martin, step into the study with me?" His stepfather threw his napkin down with disgust and retreated to his private dominion.

Margaret moved her chair back as the footman deftly pulled it away. "I will have coffee in the salon. You will join me?" she asked her husband sweetly.

"As soon as I finish my cigar, my dear. Martin?"

"Yes, sir."

The library was in the older part of the house and once belonged to an illustrious ancestor of his stepfather. He was a preacher that came over soon after the *Mayflower*, and his stepfather took every opportunity to remind everybody and

The Hanging Tree

anybody of his impressive pedigree. Martin had read about him in the local library. The reverend had made a name for himself in these parts as a 'witchfinder'. He sounded like a pompous bully, his sermons were weak, and, Martin thought smugly, were he his ancestor, he wouldn't be so eager to share it with anyone. Well, to each his own. He had his own problems. After his father's suicide, his mother had languished just on the outside of fashionable society. He had left them near penniless, and if not for her remarriage, Martin knew he'd be out on the streets looking for work or, at the very least, in the army. There was a war in Europe. It was a matter of time before the United States joined in. He wanted to be there front and center, not playing at boys' games in a fancy school with other children of the rich. He longed to go out there and make a difference. Aside from that, as long as he was far from home, his secret was safe.

"What is all this nonsense?" His stepfather lit a fat cigar. He played with the match, drawing in great gulps until the end caught, glowing nicely. The room filled with a pleasant aroma. He offered one to Martin, who declined. "They're good. Better get used to them, my boy. Don't want anyone to think you're a nancy boy."

Martin turned around and looked straight at his stepfather's heavy face. "Just what do you mean by that, sir?" he demanded icily.

The older man laughed. "Nothing. It's all about image. When you work at the firm, you have to do what everybody else is doing: play golf, smoke cigars... Why, my boy?"

Martin didn't answer. There was the rattle and clink of ice, and Martin poured his stepfather a whiskey. The lambent light from the golden glow of a Tiffany shade bathed the room with serenity. Only Martin didn't feel serene. He was agitated as well as angry. He did not want his life mapped out for him. He wanted to draw the map of his life freehand. He wanted to make it up as he went along. "I am not your boy, sir."

The older man shrugged. "I know you're angry, but Margaret doesn't want you to go. Look," he held his gaze with arctic blue eyes, "I personally don't care one way or the other. You can go be cannon fodder for all it's worth. I won't have your mother worried. She's delicate." He paused, taking a long pull on the cigar. "And in a delicate state of health."

There was the crux of the matter. Margaret had conceived with his stepfather, very late in life. Childless, he was thrilled at the prospect of an heir. No one was allowed to disturb his wife's peace of mind. "You'll do whatever she wants, whenever she wants," he held up his hands as if to stop him, "until the baby is born. We can revisit this in six months, and if you are still fired up to go slog in the mud, fighting the Huns, I will do whatever I can to get you there."

The door opened, and his butler entered. "Mrs. Harmond is getting tired. She asks for you to join her in the drawing room for coffee, sir."

"And so we shall. Martin?"

"So how did you end up here?" Gibson girl broke the silence from her branch. The two men were huddled close, the past a painful subject for both of them.

"Instead of cannon fodder, he became fertilizer," Arthur joked, to the merriment of the spirits in the tree.

"Oh, LMAO," Martin responded dryly.

"What?" Goody Bennett croaked from her spot.

The Hanging Tree

"Very funny. It's what they all write on their phones. Watch, she's doing it now." He pointed an elegant hand at Arielle.

"Gimme that." Chad tried to grab her phone. "What are you writing? LMAO? Why? Who are you texting?"

"Nobody." Arielle let him have the phone. "I was responding to my sister. If you have to know, it's because she was writing about something my father's girlfriend did."

"She's hot." Chad threw the phone back into her lap. He edged closer, pulling her into his arms, making another attempt to finish what they had started.

"What do you mean? Her ass is soooo big."

Chad pulled her down so she rested on his shoulder, their faces gazing at the stars peeking through the leafy canopy. "The bigger the tush, the better the push," he replied.

This caused Goody Bennett to laugh so hard she almost spilled out of her perch. When Gibson girl innocently asked where they would be pushing, she fell forward, startling the cat and causing the branch to sway as if in a storm.

"Oh, my God." Arielle's eyes opened wide. "Did you see that?"

Since Chad was busily unbuttoning her shirt, he had missed their close encounter with the old witch. "See what?" he asked lazily, his lips tracing the delicate skin at the base of her neck.

"Really, Chad, the branch almost bent in half."

"Wind," he murmured as he covered her mouth for a searing kiss.

Arielle loved the smell of him. She rubbed her face against his sweatshirt. Maybe she should just get the whole thing over with.

"Are you going to let this happen?" Gibson girl demanded, her eyes glued to the seduction. She felt agitated. Wringing her hands, she shifted in her perch and watched the groping couple.

"Bain't none o' my business," Goody huffed. "If she keeps going on, in another hour or two, won't matter much a'tall."

"Why? What do you know?" the younger girl demanded. A faint curtain of grey mist surrounded her, and her view became obstructed. Though she craned her skeletal neck, she could see nothing.

"I know what I know, and what I want to know is what made young Martin here an extension of yonder branch." Goody changed the subject. If she couldn't move the girl, she would do her best to preserve her innocence, or what was left of it. She puffed away on her pipe and let the smoke curl around the branches of the tree.

"Oh, you know already, Goody Bennett. It's all your fault." Martin called back.

"Here we go again, always blaming the fat girl," Goody teased back as she sucked on her pipe, her eyes black pits.

"Goody Bennett," Arthur offered, "I see you more pleasantly plump rather than fat, my dear."

"You charmer, Artie! Such a waste." Goody levitated near him. "If you had a cheek, I would pinch it."

Martin

Harvard University, 1916

"I hate it here." Martin worried the ring of the blind that dangled from his dorm window. He had lost the gangly teen look and had filled out more like a man. His wide shoulders filled the small dorm room. Impatiently, he brushed his dark, tangled hair from his high forehead. He wasn't handsome, but his face had an angular grace, his long nose gave him a regal air.

"It could be worse," Arthur replied from his bed. "We could actually have to work for a living." Arthur's whipcord frame was stretched across the bed. He had long legs that had earned him the nickname "stork". He thought himself rather dapper. Everything about him was neat, from the perfect crease in his pants, to the straight part in his short hair. He sported a thin mustache these days, to the amusement of all his fellow classmates. A year older than Martin, he felt immeasurably wiser than most anybody in his circle.

"You just have to graduate and then go work for your grandfather." Martin replied without looking at his friend.

"You think I am looking forward to that?" Arthur sat up. "You think that'll be easy? M'older brother is a boy wonder.

As if I can compete with that. If you didn't take my test for me, I never would have passed."

Martin waved his hand, dismissing what he did. "Nobody knows."

"I know." Arthur sat up on the edge of the bed, his head hanging. He combed a hand though his perfect hair leaving it disordered. A comma of it hung seductively over his green eyes. He looked up at Martin. "You can't go out and do my work for me when we graduate. I don't know what I am going to do." He stood and paced the small room. "I wish I'd never have to leave here."

"I can't wait to leave here. I want to go there." Martin pointed east.

"Where?" Arthur came to the window.

"Oh, Europe?" He placed his hand on Martin's shoulder, caressing him. "I don't know what I will do if I can't see you everyday. Martin…" he stood behind him, " You can't go to Europe, I would die if something happened to you."

Martin turned toward his roommate, their arms around each other. "We won't be able to be like this when we get out of here," he whispered fiercely.

Arthur simply pulled the shade and closed out the world.

Peter

The television bathed the room in blues and greens. "Pete," Belinda warned, "if you press the clock button one more time, I am out of here." Belinda held out her hand for the remote.

"It's after ten."

"She's seventeen. Relax. She's a good kid."

"She was," Peter replied despondently.

Belinda sat up. "Listen, she's annoyed about me."

"What are you talking about? She told me she likes you."

Belinda smiled at him. "Yeah, sure. I'd feel the same way. She's feeling displaced. You were all hers, and now she has to share. It's normal."

"How do you know?" Peter stood, pacing the room. "It's like I don't know her anymore. She's so secretive."

"And what were you doing when you were seventeen? Did you share everything with your parents?" Belinda sat forward, her eyes dancing. She reached out for him. She was just on the edge of chubby. He didn't mind, it was more to hug and made him feel safe and comfortable. He thought her pretty, though he knew his friends did snicker a bit about her size. Amy, his ex was a perfect size two, and where did that get him. He teased the brown hair from her face and kissed her softly on her lips. She smiled invitingly, but he wasn't finished talking.

Peter sat back down and pulled her into his arms. She cuddled close. "It was different. My parents were old. They didn't understand me."

Raising a delicate brow, she looked at his handsome face. She brushed back his chestnut hair and kissed him full on the lips.

"They weren't cool," he told her.

"And you are? Listen, kiddo, you're forty-four, close to retirement, divorced." She patted the slight paunch he'd recently developed. "How do you think they see you?"

"I was in a band!"

"Yeah, twenty-six years ago. Face it. You're over the hill. You have to reinvent your relationship with her. Maybe she wants a dad and not a friend."

Peter reached behind them for his telephone and said grimly, "I'm just going to check up on her. Again."

Martin

Oyster Bay, 1916

"Dinner is at eight," Margaret told her son. "Arthur and I have plans."

"Plans?" His stepfather looked up from his newspaper.

"Yes. We're meeting a group of guys from the school," Martin told them absently.

"Who?"

"Senator Raynor's son, Bill Wolfson, and—"

"Larry Merstine," Arthur added.

"The Jew?" His mother looked up from her knitting.

"Are you sure you want to go with him? I mean he can't join our club." A frown appeared on her smooth brow. "His people are not asking you to vouch for them?" she asked with alarm. She had gained weight with this pregnancy and her double chin wobbled.

Martin didn't answer her but made a dismissive sound. He hated it when she was like this. If she didn't tolerate other religions, just imagine her reaction if she found out about his preferences. Holy hell would break loose. He smiled as he stared out the window. "What's so funny, darling?" she asked him.

His stepfather's booming voice interrupted before he could think of an appropriate answer. "His father is important," Mr. Harmond added. "He owns Merstine Mercantile. They've expanded into twelve states. Giving the five and dime a run for the money."

"Parvenus." Arthur added as he smirked to Mrs. Harmond, who responded with a smile. She liked this young man her son brought home. She was hoping he'd notice Eugenie but no such luck. He was charming and an absolutely clever dancer.

"Such grace," she'd told her husband. Yes, he was a good influence on her wayward son. "Upstarts," she agreed with a nod.

Eugenie burst into the room. "What have you done with her?" she demanded from her stepfather. "What have you done to my cat?"

"Eugenie, apologize this instant!" Margaret yelled hotly.

"I don't know where that flea-bitten beast is." He looked at Martin and winked conspiratorially. "The creature's got more lives than any cat I know." He laughed at his own joke.

"What are you talking about?" Martin asked.

"He took my cat and drove her out east and left her to *die*!" Eugenie circled the room, her voice filled with venom. "She will find her way home. She always finds her way home. Oh, I hate you!" She fled the room, slamming the door in a fury of lace and flowered chiffon.

Later that night, Martin and Arthur sat by the tennis courts drinking gin and tonics. "I don't know why you drink this swill." Arthur took out a small flask from his suit pocket.

Martin declined the offer of whiskey. "Rotgut. I like the more civilized drinks."

The Hanging Tree

Arthur admired the lean lines of Martin's silhouette as he leaned on the fence post. He was so incredibly good looking it caused a flutter deep in his chest every time he gazed at his lover's face.

Arthur laughed. "What happened to the cat?"

"Oh, my stepfather abhors the animal. Tried to get rid of it, but the thing keeps returning here."

Arthur looked back at the elegant mansion behind them. "Can't say I blame her. He can't stand you either."

"Hates my guts." Martin said grimly.

Arthur leaned closer to hear Martin's muted whisper "I think he knows," he confided.

Arthur's stomach clenched. He might have looked devil-may-care, but all hell would break loose if his father found out. Disinheriting was a real threat, and he knew it. "I'd have to kill him if he knew." Arthur stood nervously and laughed. He stomped his long legs, as if they had fallen asleep. His white teeth gleamed in the darkness, but Martin knew his friend was not smiling.

"You are kidding?" Martin leaned so close their breaths touched. They laced their fingers together.

"Do you think he'll say anything?"

Martin shrugged. "It gives him leverage. Look, all I want is a ticket out of here. I am afraid."

"Of what?" Arthur gripped Martin's hand tighter.

"I am afraid the fighting will stop and I would have missed it," he whispered urgently.

"Are you so eager to get yourself killed?" Arthur released their hands and grabbed him by the lapels of his tux, his face white in the moonlight. "I love you. I can't live without you. You can't go!"

"This thing is bigger than us." Martin turned away, his eyes distant.

Arthur was going to lose him. He knew it, deep in his heart; he knew their time was running short. "What are you talking about? Nothing is bigger than us." Arthur started walking back to the house. "I thought this year meant something to you." He ran a shaking hand through his hair. "All you ever cared about was the war. I'm sick of hearing about the stupid war. I mean it. I'm sick of it, Marty."

"Don't call me Marty!"

Arthur walked away. Martin never turned to see him leave. He watched the night sky, wondering if it looked the same on the battlefields of France.

"You never got to go, did you?" Gibson girl asked quietly.

"I never left Long Island again." Martin looked up at the unchanging heavens.

Peter

"Where do you think they are?" They drove past the movie theater.

"Let's go to Friendly's. Maybe they went for ice cream. We could drive past the diner again. Gimme your phone. I'll see if she answers." Belinda took his cell and punched in Arielle's number. Peter could hear her voicemail answer and his neck turned red with anger.

"I'm going to kill her. We have a rule: you always answer your phone." Peter was steaming.

"Maybe the battery's dead."

Peter gripped the wheel tighter and turned the car toward the diner.

Arielle

"Okay, stop. I'm done!"

"I'm not!" Chad held her captive; her shoulders were pinned to the ground.

"I changed my mind." She struggled against him, and he placed his leg over her, imprisoning her.

"It's too late for that." Chad's tone was harsh, his breathing labored.

"Are you kidding me?" Arielle raised her voice. "Who are you?" she demanded. His eyes gleamed in the moonlight; his hands became aggressive, one holding her wrists together, the other tearing at her shirt. She opened her mouth, but her scream was cut short by Chad's mouth. He roughly pulled her shirt free of her tight jeans.

"You're a tease, Arielle." He placed his lips on her mouth, absorbing the sound again. Arielle kicked against him, but he was stronger, his work at the gym a sure advantage.

"Are you going to let him get away with that?" Gibson girl gravitated off her branch, her voice high and agitated. She looked at Goody wildly. "It's what they did to *me*. Please, Goody, make him stop!" she pleaded. She placed her hands on her thin chest, knowing that Arielle's heartbeat would be wild like a caged bird as well. Sniffing, she howled long and hard as memories hit her with tidal force. She kept repeating, "make them stop…make them *stop*…"

"I didn't mean for that to happen to you," Goody said sadly. "The whole thing got out of hand. You were in the wrong place at the wrong time."

"But I had the right name!" Gibson girl said hotly, her eyes glowing red in the darkness with hurt and anger, she continued acidly, "Muriel Harmond! And you let them do those evil things to me. It has to stop. You have to stop him. You…" Muriel pointed a finger at the old, cunning woman, "…you are making him do this!"

It was a tense moment in the tree, and the air vibrated with hatred mixed with anxiety.

They all knew about Gibson girl. They never made her retell her story. It made them all so sad, even Claire, and she didn't feel pity for anybody. They all watched Chad overpower Arielle on the ground, his hips grinding into hers. She struggled mightily against him, to no avail.

"Well, he is an asshole, Grandmother." Claire nodded toward the struggling couple.

"Oh, aye, that he is. What will it be?"

"Something to scare the shit out of him," Arthur added helpfully.

Goody Bennett, the strongest of the souls, squeezed her eyes shut and concentrated. She pictured a ball of flame in the center of her chest and felt it expand. The heat rose, and so did she become a giant tornado of flame. Whirling toward Chad's unsuspecting back, she rammed him hard, slamming down the length of him. His breath whooshed out of his body, and he rolled off Arielle, who used the opportunity to scramble up.

The Hanging Tree

"What'd you hit me with?" He turned on her, breathing hard.

Arielle's eyes opened wide as a wall of flame danced around them. She felt the searing heat come close to her face, but it merely warmed her, not harming her. Chad's clothes, however, smoked in spots. Reaching out, she touched the flame and watched it caress her arm.

Chad reached out, slapping her arm. "Stop that! Ow!" The fire bit his skin, singeing him.

Swirling into a cyclone, it spun upward in a spiral until it disappeared into a puff of smoke.

Both teenagers watched it rise until it popped into a starburst not unlike a grand firework display. "Did you see that? What was that?" Chad looked at the dispersing smoke.

"I don't know, and I don't care. I'm leaving. Lose my number, Chad."

"Brava, Arielle," Claire's hoarse voice whispered.

"You know you wanted it, Arielle. You said as much last week."

"I don't know what I saw in a loser like you," Arielle answered hotly.

"So you're saying you don't want to be with me?" Chad asked incredulously.

"Bing-fucking-o! I'm outta here." Arielle turned to walk home.

"Stop, Arielle. I'll drive you home." His voice was contrite. He didn't know what had come over him. He felt like two different people, and one was someone he didn't know too well. He was feeling limp, defeated, as if the wind had left his sails. His face reddened and he was ashamed of how aggressive he felt a minute ago. It was wrong, and he didn't know how to explain what had happened to him.

"I am not getting into that car with you ever again." Arielle turned her back on him.

"Fine. I thought you wanted it. You give mixed messages," Chad shot back as a car's headlights turned into the lane. He didn't want the blame to fall on him. It wasn't fair, he thought petulantly.

The cat was back, winding its body around Arielle. "Help me find my phone, pretty kitty." She felt around in the dark, looking for her cell.

Headlights lit the area as a car pulled up. Arielle shielded her eyes, trying to see who it was. "Leo!" Chad called. "Did you see that?"

"What?" the youth called back without getting out of the car. "I didn't see nuthin'. Did you do it?" He nodded at Arielle.

Chad made a negative sound.

"Oh, was I too early?" Leo asked with a smirk.

"Forget about it. Let's do this." Chad dusted off his pants and walked to his car. "You stay here." He pointed to her. "I was going to have you ride with me but forget it. I'll take you home, and we'll talk later."

"I have nothing to say to you, Chad," Arielle said primly.

"Have it your way." He shrugged, knowing she'd forgive him. She'd have to; he was Chad Harmond, the most desirable boy in the school. He smiled as he jumped into the Camaro. "Start at the top of the fork. First one to where One-oh-six intersects wins."

"Oh, no, here we go again. Goody, can you stop this madness?" Martin whispered. "Weren't we enough for you? I'm not even a Harmond."

"I never thought about that." Muriel looked up, her face tear-stained. "Why did you let them crash?"

Martin And Arthur

Oyster Bay, 1916

"Slow down, Arthur!" Martin yelled as they took the turn onto Route 106 too fast.

Arthur drank deeply from his flask. "What are you, afraid?" his voice slurred. "This is how they drive the army ambulances in France. Don't you want to get used to it?" he taunted.

Martin reached for the wheel, and the two men struggled for control. The headlights lit up the dark street with puddles of light. Both their brains felt fuzzy with alcohol.

"Watch out!" Arthur shouted as a black cat raced in front of them. It paused, arching its back and screeched loudly. Its eyes glowed like a jack-o-lantern, pinning them so that their backs pressed into the leather upholstery. He felt two wheels lift off the ground, and the car rolled over. As if in slow motion, Martin opened his mouth to scream, but the sound was cut off as their necks snapped; followed by their chests crushing into the interior seats as the car flipped over and over until they rested up against an oak tree. Immobile, they were trapped on the ground, body parts strewn around the tree base. Dazed, they looked at each other, not quite understanding what had just happened. A cackle shook the tree, and the two spied an old crone looking down at them.

"Welcome aboard, fellas!" she said gleefully.

"But you still didn't tell me why," Muriel wailed. "I don't understand why?"

"Just look," Claire offered gently and gestured to the night sky, where their stories played out.

The smoking wreck lay in a crumbled heap, the bodies unrecognizable. It was daybreak, and a police car was parked to the side. An officer stood writing notes, measuring tire burns on the single lane. A long limousine with a chauffeur pulled up as the sun lit the sky.

"Don't get out, Margaret!" his stepfather ordered.

It was too late. Margaret Harmond staggered out of the car, falling to her knees beside her son's twisted body. "Martin…" she wept, trying to hold his head. It was listless in her arms, his eyes sightless, his limbs at unnatural angles. "Oh, my son, my Martin. What have you done?" Gasping, she fell forward, blood seeping from her skirts. Grabbing her belly, she cried out, "The baby!"

"Margaret!" her husband wailed, his dreams and hers bleeding onto the black road.

"You took revenge on him because of his stepfather's child?" Muriel said quietly.

"A curse is a curse. I don't pick it. They did. I didn't drive fast. They did. I didn't wander the dark roads. You did."

"I was following the cat!" Muriel shrieked.

"It was your own free will. The curse found you," the older woman told her.

"You have to stop this!" Muriel stood, facing her. "This is madness. This is evil."

"Out of the question. I am spent. Aside from that, they're too far away already." Goody Bennett turned her face away from the girl.

Arielle

Arielle eyed the tree warily, moving away. Twin headlights moved down the road, the cars racing to see who would win. She heard them honking playfully and just wanted the evening to be over. Once she found her phone, she was calling her father and letting him know he was absolutely right: Chad was a jerk. It was strange; they were distantly related, shared the same grandfather way back in the Middle Ages or something. Her father said they were like ninth cousins. She had told him she didn't even have to change her name if they married. Wouldn't that be neat? Arielle Harmond she was, and Arielle Harmond she'd remain. She bit a short fingernail and wondered if that was the real attraction.

The cars moved forward, their engines revving in the night; she could hear them shifting to higher speeds. They were closer; she could even see that they were playing chicken with each other, moving close, as if to brush against the other, but moving away recklessly. Boys were just stupid. *What is this supposed to accomplish?* she wondered.

Another car was coming down the street in the opposite direction. It was a Jeep Cherokee, a white one. "Dad," she whispered, knowing she was in deep shit now. He saw her from his window and turned the car, sharply heading toward her. The two cars were moving very fast now, caught up in their race. Her father's vehicle was making a left into their trajectory path. Arielle's breath caught in her throat.

Time stopped for a moment; the air was turgid, still, too thick to draw breath. She heard a faint cackle of laughter from the tree, followed by a frantic meow.

Arielle saw the cat move into the center of the street, into the path of all three cars.

She could see her father's white face, his mouth caught in a rictus of horror, Belinda's eyes frozen on her. In the other direction, Leo's horn blared as he pressed it relentlessly, telling everyone to move out of the way. Lastly she saw Chad's face, his arms battling for control of the wheel. Time stood still. Leaping nimbly, she moved into the middle of the street. The light around them had taken on an odd glow; everything looked dusted with gold. Sound had disappeared, and she felt enveloped in a vacuum. It was foolish, running onto this main road, but Arielle knew she had to. The cat locked her gleaming eyes on her and without reservation, she walked toward her in the street. She held her arms out, reaching for the frozen cat, grabbing it while making eye contact with her father, forcing him to swerve onto the median so he would miss her. He collided with the speed sign. The hood of his car crumbled; air bags deployed.

She stood perfectly still, two racing cars on either side of her, their horns blaring. Willing herself small, she held her breath, closed her eyes. She felt the vibration of their movement, the speed burning her cheeks, the horns screaming in unison. The air prickled her bare arms as the cars rushed past her, her hair flaring like a halo around her face.

The Hanging Tree

Muriel would have released a breath if she had one, suddenly free, she hopped down from her branch to join Claire at the base of the tree.

Goody glided off her perch, her wrinkled face wreathed with a peaceful smile.

She gravitated above Arielle, her hands reaching out to caress her head. "You saved her. You saved my Remedy."

Arthur and Martin jumped from their perch, imprisoned no longer. Their bodies were whole, as if they were never mangled on the branch. Arthur brushed the wrinkles from his raccoon coat. "Marty, Remedy was the remedy," Arthur laughed.

"Don't call me Marty," his friend replied with a smile and tweaked the comma of hair that hung over Arthur's forehead.

Arthur smiled back rakishly, his handsome face restored. He patted down his perfect trousers, reached over and took the goggles from Martin's face. "Much better, you look like yourself, you old thing." His boyish smile lit up his handsome face.

"She saved my cat. She saved my cat," the old woman crooned.

Arielle petted the purring cat, her eyes watching the two cars as their taillights disappeared down the street. She turned to look at her father, her eyes shining. "Don't say anything, Dad. You okay? Hi, Belinda." She ran toward her father, who was inspecting the smoking front end of his car.

"If I ever see you—"

"Don't say it, Daddy." He was a sucker when she called him that. "You were right. I won't see him again. Did you get hurt?" She ran into his arms.

"Did you?" He grabbed her and held her tight, the cat cuddled between the two of them. It meowed in distress and they separated. "What are you doing here?"

"We were just hanging out. I was looking for my phone to call and ask you to pick me up. He's not the right boy for me."

Her father looked at her and opened his mouth.

"Enough said, Peter." Belinda walked over to them from the side of the car. "I told you you could trust her. See if you can drive the car. Let's go home."

"Wait a minute." Arielle crossed the street to put the cat gently on the ground beneath the tree. "Thank you for helping." She paused before the large oak, searching the branches. Something was there, she was sure of it, she couldn't see them, but that didn't mean anything, she knew that now.. She called out to the foliage, "I know you're there. I think I can feel you." The air was pulsing with something she didn't understand, but it made her aware of every hair on her head. In fact, she felt the small hairs stand up on her arms as well. She shivered involuntarily, her eyes scanning for any movement.

She watched the tree shake a bit, and the outline of an old lady appeared. She looked to be embedded in the tree, as if her wrinkled face was part of the bark. Smiling benignly, she said, "One good deed deserves another. Thank you for saving my cat." It was a mere whisper, but Arielle heard it and grinned.

Chad's car pulling up behind her, she recognized it from its noisy muffler. The headlights lit the entire area. Chad jumped out and walked to her side. They turned to face each other. Arielle glanced and saw Belinda hold out her hand to stay her father, who was spoiling for a fight with the younger man.

The Hanging Tree

"I'm sorry I led you on. I'm not ready for this." Arielle smiled at him sadly.

"I don't know what came over me. I'm sorry." They spoke at the same time and laughed.

"Let's be friends." Chad held out his hand.

"Kissing cousins." Arielle touched his cheek, waved goodbye, and walked across the street to her father.

"Well, what are we waiting for?" Arthur asked.

"It's over," Martin responded.

"Abraca-fucking-dabra." Claire glided over to them.

"Claire, watch thy tongue!" her grandmother admonished.

"I still don't understand what happened," Muriel wailed.

"Oh, stop your caterwauling," Claire responded. "There was a curse."

"Aye, don't go blaming my curse. It only worked when you put yourself in danger." The old woman was lighting a pipe.

"Goody," Arthur called out, "haven't you heard that smoking will kill you?"

"I'm going to miss you, Artie. You, too, Marty." They were already beginning to fade.

"Why were we here?" Muriel persisted.

"Trapped by the curse on Harmond. Watch." Claire pointed to the sky.

All around her, familiar souls, relations of the ill-fated Harmond clan, began their journeys to freedom. She heard the howls of relief as they moved gracefully to a better place.

"Why?" Muriel turned to Claire. She recognized many of her relatives.

"A Harmond caused the curse, and a Harmond released the curse. The girl saved my cat. She risked her own life to save someone dear to me." Goody Bennett's face was fading, her features softening in the early morning light.

The sun rose high, warming the earth, bathing the flowers with light and love. Muriel Harmond found peace at last too.

Author's Note

Oyster Bay was first settled by the Dutch in 1639, Anchoring their ships in a large Long Island bay, it was named for the plentiful and delicious oysters found there. The English settled in the area around 1653. It served as a haven for Quaker's fleeing religious persecution from New Amsterdam. Clearly my group of imaginary settlers would not have lived there yet. To my knowledge, there were no witch-hunts, hangings, or burnings in the area.

There is a legend of a 'hanging tree' in the area. It is an overgrown oak that was the scene of a horrific accident in the early years of the 20th century on Route 107 in East Norwich. It is said when the light is just right, you can see and hear the victims sprawled in the branches of the tree. I have been there, and yes, it gives me the creeps.

Follow Michael

@michaelpcash

www.michaelphillipcash.com

If you find this book enjoyable, I really hope you'll leave a review on Amazon under The Hanging Tree. If you have any questions or comments, please contact me directly at **michaelphillipcash@gmail.com**.

About the Author

Born and raised on Long Island, Michael has always had a fascination with horror writing and found footage films. Earning a degree in English and an MBA, he has worked various jobs before settling into being a full-time author. He currently resides on Long Island with his wife and children.

michaelphillipcash@gmail.com

BONUS!

First two chapters from my new Space Opera
Schism: The Battle for Darracia
Chapter 1

"Pay attention, your highness." The navigator implored the disinterested young man who gazed out of the wall of windows. "Prince V'sair please... your father had demanded." The teacher pointed to the mathematical example that hung mid air, ignored and not solved. He raised his arm reluctantly, and the numbers dissolved instantly to be replaced by a history lesson. The lad loved that subject, surely he would finish something today!

The teen turned, his blazing white hair a nimbus around his lean, wolf like face. He was a handsome male, whipcord lean, with a high forehead, and bright blue eyes that studied his tutor with growing disdain.

"Emmicus, my head aches with your numbers and sums. I know the speed of time, inside and out. I can calculate the distance to travel to Fon Reni get our mid meal and be home in time for chay with my mother. I am weary of this."

The older man approached his young charge, sympathy in his rheumy eyes. "Yes, yes, I know, your highness, your wit is brighter than our own Rast," he bowed his head reverently and watched the boy do the same as they repeated together,

"Great Sradda, giver of all life and love, we commend ourselves to thee."

Together they made an arc of their forefingers that touched the breastbone of their chest. There was a minute of silence, so thick the air vibrated and the tutor, lost in prayer, failed to see the younger man looking up and out the giant, clear wall again. He heard the sigh, and climbed out of his peaceful state. The boy was not himself today, the pained look was in his face once again. He loved this man-child as if he had sprung from his own loins and had been given the charge of him from the time he left his mother's womb. He had taught him to dress, read, fight, ride the wild stallius, tamed for only the noble class and royalty. He had taught him to wipe his own ass, and then his nose, making sure he didn't contaminate the two.

Gently, he tried again, "V'sair, what is it my son?" he asked kindly, moving close to him for privacy. Though they were alone in the room, their voices sometimes carried throughout the great auditorium.

The prince looked at his elderly teacher. How to say it without hurting him? Emmicus had protected him from his father's wrath when he failed to do his work and hid him when his uncle played his dirty power games.

He was a half breed, the only one in the Kingdom of Darracia. Was it his fault his father, the King Drakko had

The Hanging Tree

traveled to Planta as a young man and married the first female he had seen there? His father defied his tribe, cast aside his betrothed, his royal oath and taken for a wife, the orange tattooed daughter of his grandfather's greatest enemy. He had found her on a mission to Planta, a world where many of the Darracian warriors met a watery death in its boundless ocean. Drakko fought and won the heart of Reminda, princess of Adon, the lush island surrounded by a great, green sea. He had stolen her away, first fighting her father and then his own, to be with her. It was his greatest battle, and she his favorite prize of war.

V'sair was a freak. While his father had the pebbled gray skin of the Darracian race, his skin was tan, with a hint of blue to match the silvery blue eyes he'd inherited from his mother. Built like his mother, he was long limbed and graceful looking, not nearly as tall as the rest of the male Darracians. His skin was smooth and hairless, making him feel like a pet rather than an offspring. He knew his father loved him as fiercely as he loved his mother, but did he trust him? Did he have faith in his abilities? A boy, nay a man of his age should have learned the Secrets of the Sradda. The ceremony was long overdue and did not look to ever occur. He was older than many of his cousins, yet he had not been given the Fireblade, or spent the night locked with the elders learning the lesson that would turn him into a warrior. It was a right of passage that marked a Darracian man's journey to adulthood. It was as if a club was created and he was not allowed in. He was no better than the Quyroo, imprisoned on the Desa, left to live in the treetops to hunt and forage for food many miles from his kingdom.

"I might as well color my skin red and braid my hair," he muttered angrily.

"Nonsense young sir! Nonsense…" the older man followed and placed a warm hand on his shoulder. "You are royal born!" He caught V'sair's angry glare.

"No one can take that away from you. You are the descendant of the most high Darracian, Carnor the First. His life force strums in your veins."

"Pah. I am equally the product of my mother's clan."

"Less so, V'sair! You have been brought up here among wealth and knowledge. You have studied hard and know the Sradda Doctrines better than anyone else. You are as brave as you are smart. I am proud to have you as a pupil."

"Only you see it Emmicus. The Secrets, I want to take part in the ceremony. I fear they will never let me take up the Fireblade. I am being left behind. They are going to make me a…a navigator." His face blushed blue when he realized he insulted his best ally. "I mean… there's nothing wrong with being a navigator, it's an important job, Emmicus.."

"V'sair, V'sair, stop. I know you are not meant to be a scholar." He turned the younger man to face him. "You are a warrior, with a warrior's life-force, Great Sradda willing," they both bowed their heads respectfully. "Your time will come. I know, but for now, how about we recite the Sradda? If you won't do my lessons, then give your old navigator some pleasure and tell me about the creation."

V'sair looked at the hope lighting his teacher's face. The Sradda Doctrine was just a jumble of words to him now. He had prayed for years and had been denied the one thing he wanted more than anything else. He'd rather be out, riding Hother, the purebred stallius his mother had presented him just last year. He loved to bury his face in the white velvet neck, then take off and glide through the atmosphere, holding

The Hanging Tree

on for dear life. Hother flew above the treetops, her hooves sparking with energy when they landed.

He thought he should abdicate for his older half-brother. If only they would let him. Zayden was full-blooded Darracian, and one of the best warriors in the army. Anyone would be happy to follow him, the plain fact of his illegitimacy making it impossible to inherit. V'sair was destined to be the future king whether he wanted it or not. He opened his mouth to complain, but when he saw Emmicus's eager face, he began the first calls to the Sradda Doctrine, hoping the melodious cadence of the tale of his ancestors, his birthright, would calm his aching heart. He walked around the vast chamber, his booted feet making scuffing sounds on the polished floor. It was a huge room and he moved to position himself, so that his voice would echo from the vaulted ceiling. He knew this room in and out, had studied there with Emmicus for almost everyday of his nineteen years. He was way past the age for a schoolroom, most of his boyhood friends and cousins had already taken their places in the army. He frowned, knowing he rode better than any of them, his lithe frame made him agile, and fast, their Darracian bulk weighing them down. He opened his mouth, and instead of the first prayer, he continued his argument as if they had never stopped. "I disagree with my father, Emmicus. You know I could hold my own against any of my cousins, I know I could." He implored his tutor.

Emmicus bowed his craggy head, "It is true, you have Planta agility. You are fleet of foot," he moved close to the younger man and tapped the smooth forehead with his wrinkled finger. "It's what is here that is important, V'sair. You have to be able to outwit your enemy." V'sair pulled away angrily. He moved his finger to the boy's heaving chest and touched the area over his heart, gently, "You have to use tools other than brawn to lead. Your father and I have discussed this. If you are to command, you must do it with your heart and soul and mind. Anyone can fight, V'sair! This trinity with the Elements alone will make you a leader. The greatest in the history of Darracia. Now, if you please… the Song of Sradda."

V'sair looked up at the ceiling, not knowing if his voice would crack with emotion. He was frustrated with Emmicus, his father and the entire planet. Putting his hand on the cold pane of glass overlooking the cloud city, he began, his voice a whisper, "The Three Elements were designed by the Creator. Molded from veriest ether, He grew them from the nothingness of space, to pulse with the knowledge of the ages to bring life to all our worlds. Lovingly formed, with noble intention, they were dispatched by the Creator." Here he bowed his head as he was taught to do, making the arc of life from his fingers to his breastbone, his voice growing stronger, more confident, the words vibrating thought his heart, his mouth reciting the words, but his thoughts on the elusive Fireblade. Emmicus watchfully mirrored him. "The one who created our living Universe." A five millisecond pause, and he began again. "It was up to these three Elements to leave behind a Universe of tranquility and order. While they were created for the good of all-kind, one must earn it, work for it, for the Creator brings the spark only to those that deserve it. These are the tools, the conduit and I shall name them…Ozre,"

Emmicus chanted after him, "Ozre, Ozre Light the path…"

The Hanging Tree

V'sair continued, "Ozre, Ozre light the path...Ozre, oh, great Element of Earth. Ozre who swirled the dust in its path and with this the rocks were created. The rocks were heated into stars, the stars gave birth to planets. Joining like particles of life in the air, they began their orbit, and Ozer was happy. Ozer's joy begat Ereth, Ereth...giver of life."

Again the older man repeated the refrain, his eyes an odd glow of one wrapped in prayer, lost in the moment of deep thought. V'sair noted it with a smile, but continued the ritual, knowing he was so very well trained and his voice filled the room. He was a good Yoman, a born speaker who could call people to prayer and make the unbelievers holy once more. If only it worked for him.

"Ereth, the Element of water, giver of oceans and lakes and rivers to divide the lands. To make the Desa grow. To create the waters for the spark of life to grow. And Ereth's joy begat Ine."

"Ozre begat Ereth, Ereth begat Ine, Ine mother of life..." Emmicus was swaying, his body vibrating lost in the pleasure of prayer.

"Ine, the Element of Life, giver of the planets their seed of life. The first breath of existence as we know. Creator to Ozre to Ereth to Ine, one is powerless without the other. Each connected with the spirit of life. One without the other is not whole. The Trivium is whole. The Elements are whole."

His voice soared to the eaves of the great ceiling, his bell like tenor filling the chamber with the music of Darracian soul. Detached, he watched Emmicus, his tutor's face rapt with the music of the words, knowing he affected the older man deeply. He wished the words could do the same for him.

While he recited with all the passion that the navigator had immersed into him, the prayers meant nothing. He longed to understand what others felt, and wondered if his tainted blood played a role. Though his voice was rich, he felt empty. Perhaps he was not really Darracian.

He continued softly, "And the Creator left behind his most important gift. The Trivium, our Elements. Though He is all knowing, He left these sentinels to guide us, watch us, teach us. As they moved around the newly created stars and sprinkled the seeds of life, they bathe us with their light. Each with their own color of light from the spectrum of the all-knowing. A shining orb of red, glowing hot, for the birth of strength; blue, ice cold for the reason of justice, and green; for the freedom of choice. These three spirits left behind by the Creators for us, only us, to grow, learn and be dominant. They are the Universal subconscious. They are the all-powerful. Without them we are nothing."

He just wished he could believe they were really there.

Chapter 2

The door opened and his mother entered in a flurry of flowing robes and the flowery scent she liked to wear. Her skin too was dusted blue, she was darker than her son, and she had the geometric orange tattoos in swirls over her high cheekbones. She turned her iridescent silver- blue eyes on him. They were alight with mirth when they touched gently on her son's face.

"Your Highness," Emmicus bowed his shaggy head, never to make eye contact with the King's wife.

"Arise, Navigator," she touched the top of his forehead, and he dipped in respect. "Leave us. I have need of my son." She had a musical voice that captivated one and all.

The older man bowed once again, and "I will see you after you visit, your Highness, Great Sradda willing." His heels clicked loudly on the polished, stone floor.

"Walk we me, V'sair. Come watch the setting suns."

"As you wish, Your Highness."

She paused and looked at his face, her eyes caressing his smooth skin, "What nonsense is this, Vsos," she chided him affectionately, "You used to call me 'Mo'mo.'"

"I was young, Mother," he gave in halfway, still refusing to call her by his childhood name for her.

"You are angry, Vsos. Tell me what's wrong."

They stepped toward the glass wall and as they approached, a portal opened allowing them to step onto the parapets of the vast castle. Their fortress floated above the purple clouds of the planet Darracia. Two bold suns, one fiery red, it's name was Rast, the other a duller orange, called Nost, hung low on the horizon, glowing hotly in the pewter sky. Their home was made of the red rocks of the planet, so dense and thick, it could be polished to a metal-like shine, and was as solid as it was impenetrable. The sky around them was filled with buildings, all polished to a high gloss with red glass made from the ocre sands of the Plains of Dawid. The city was vast, the buildings tall, spread out as far as the eye could see. Slowly, outlines of small colored lights popped on, defining the city skyscape, as the day was waning. Only the castle used white lights. Ramdam Crystals kept the city a mile above the red planet and separated from its less civilized inhabitants. These small crystals, a gift from the Elements, powered the entire cloud city. They were mined from the trees, on the planet by the Quyroo. Darracians lead the world and Quyroo's or the people of the trees, did the labor. Cloud City was a busy metropolis, a great financial hub. He could see singular vehicles moving from port to port, taking Darracians from their work to home. In the distance, the residential area floated in clusters over the great sea of Darracia. Air buses moved the Quyroo back to the planet after a weary day of work. They could not travel back unless Darracians powered the shuttles. It kept the two societies separate and subjugated the Quyroo to the will of the Darracians.

The Quyroo themselves were divided into two distinct groups, Tree Dwellers and Bottom Dwellers. The Tree Dwellers lived in the tall branches of the Desa forest using all

The Hanging Tree

the resources the planet had to offer. The Bottom Dwellers were often outcasts, thrown from their clans to live on the floor of the forest, eating only what they could forage.

The Darracians had built a complex city here in the clouds, many storied buildings, floating over the mountaintops, never to be touched by the unpredictability of the land.

In the distance, Aqin, the giant dormant volcano smoked sulkily. It had erupted eons ago, long before the Darracians controlled the planet. Small illegal Quyroo villages dotted it's craggy, red hills, stubbornly clinging to its rocky walls. They were forbidden to build on the sacred land of the great volcano, but many of the bottom dwellers persisted in breaking the law and tested the boundaries of Darracian patience and strength.

The Darracians were a prosperous people, wily as they were smart and ruled this planet with both their wits as well as their brawn, though many claimed it was only by the grace of the Elements alone. They had been the dominant force for over a thousand years, when his long ago ancestor, Carnor the First harnessed the power of the Elements to overcome the civil wars destroying the planet.

V'sair took in the might of his father's army and smiled, knowing that the Elements were not always on the side of the righteous, so much as on the side with the greatest warriors. Whatever his beliefs, without the support of his kingdom, his would be a hollow crown. Without the test of the Fireblade, he may not be believed mighty enough to lead these people. A heaviness rested in his chest. Darrican's respected might and despised weakness.

He looked at the army of guards lining the many towers, their granite faces, all the same dark gray of his father, with the tough pebbled skin of the Darracians, made them formidable enemies. Would they put their faith in him when the time came, he wondered. Sradda willing, he thought automatically, his father should live another two hundred years, but when the time came for him to be crowned would he have the support of these beings? A cold people, it was strange that his sire took his mother, the peaceable and pliant Planta woman as his mate.

Reading his thoughts, his mother smiled and said, "You are wondering how your father chose me?" Her forked tongue touched the tip of her full lips. He had the thick, solid tongue of his Darracian ancestors and loved trying to catch his mother's serpent like appendage when he was a child. She smiled, and her cheeks dimpled.

"It's not fair that you know all my thoughts." He had the grace to blush the palest blue. The darkening shadows painted his face violet.

"Even if I were not Planta, I would know your every thought, Vsos. You are my son." She pressed her smooth forehead against his. "Tell me of the storms are brewing behind your fine eyes."

V'sair ducked his head away, embarrassed that the guards might have seen his mother's affection. "Stop. I told you I am not a child. Am I not allowed a modicum of privacy?" He stalked down the wide terrace feeling the heat of the two suns on his face, even at this distance. If he wasn't careful, he would burn as he knew both he and his mother could not withstand the strong double rays.

"You cannot compete with the strength of the Darracians. They will destroy you." His mother calmly followed him.

The Hanging Tree

"Please lower your voice." He turned to her, wanting to keep their discussion private. "How am I to be accepted as a leader, if you won't let me take part in the Fireblade?"

"Aeeehe." She nodded with great understanding. "You worry about the Fireblade. You have no need of that. You are Drakko's son, descendant of the mighty Carnor. You are heir to the Elements. You have no need to prove yourself with the Fireblade."

"Oh no, Mo'mo," he stopped her in a rush of emotion, and she smiled at his slip from manhood. "Don't you understand? I have to take my place beside my cousins. If I don't they will never respect me. Aside from that, Zayden is equally the heir to the Elements. People would rush to his banner."

"Nonsense, V'sair. I adore Zayden, but he is just your father's byblow. He is a fine warrior and will make an able counselor to aide you, but the stain of his bastardy will never allow him kingship. What talk is this? The Darracians must respect you, you are going to be their anointed king," she chided him.

V'sair leaned against the hard balustrade of the terrace and looked out on to the whole of Darracia spread out before him. One by one, more lights from the buildings flickered on and the city in the clouds looked like diamonds strewn across a purple velvet. "I am not Darracian..."

"Oh, Voso of course…"

"Hear me out, please, Mo'mo. " He stopped her and she came up to stand next to him, her slim body buffeted by the hot winds. Shading her sensitive eyes with the delicate webbing between her fingers, from the blazing sunset, she shook her head. "Go on." She scanned the deepening sky the orange flames of the sun giving way to a mauve twilight.

"I am not like them," he gestured the hulking guard standing nearby, his dark gaze intent on the vista before them. "They don't understand my intellect. I am a hybrid. I am not Planta like you either," he showed her the corded muscles of his arm, then flexed his very individual digits, finally making a fist. He watched a smile light her face then turned to look up at the dull sky and gestured the descending suns. "Look, Mo'mo. The two suns of our planet. Rast, rich with energy, it's strength puts the weak shine of Nost to shame. Zayden and my cousins are Rast," he hung his head and she wanted to stroke his ivory haired pate. "I am the weakling, I am Nost. I am not even like the Quyroo."

"Thank the Elements for that, my son!" she said with a tinkling laugh. "Who would want to spend their day swinging from tree to tree, living in their limited world?"

"Don't you see? I am nobody. I am not acceptable for any of our species. I am an anomaly."

"You are the best of every world, a combination of all that's the finest of what we each have to offer. Your father and I have discussed this from the day you were born. You cannot compete with the Darracian might, so we have developed your intellect." She looked at him sideways, her eyes glittering. "Emmicus had retired, Dado brought him back just for you. You know he tutored your father and your uncle. You are the new Darracia. You will change this world with your will and fine mind. Bring it into the present. The Quyroo want to move into the new century as equals, they need a perceptive leader to ease the whole planet forward. Just think what you could accomplish when all species work together. Think of the medicine, science and opening trade with other planets. We can't be taken seriously in the galaxy as long as some of our inhabitants are oppressed. You are special. I have known that from the moment they put you in my arms. I have worked so hard for this and things are finally changing here..." She twirled a long strand of her white hair, until it curled charmingly around her triangular face. They stood in silence for a bit, watching the many stars begin to dot the blackness of the sky. She smoothed back her hair, taking it out of the ribbon holding at the base of her delicate neck, to fall like a cloak around her. "It's your Universe."

V'sair stared out into the horizon knowing his mother had brought the first breath of change to his land in ten thousand years. Society had fractured here, and the two species has separated, one the oppressor the other the oppressed. There had never been a thought for change until Reminda gently introduced ideas of enlightenment in her salons. Many a noble had sat at her table and with good food, wine, and conversation, she was able to slowly urge prejudice and intolerance to give way to acceptance. She had literally rocked this planet to its foundation. He looked at her serene face, loving her with all of his being. She turned to face him, a gentle smile on her lips, her elegant hand caressed his forearm. "Your suns are burning me, Vsos, I cannot stay out longer."

Proof

38019643R10065

Made in the USA
Charleston, SC
23 January 2015